Our Warfare

Three Thrilling Plays to Uncover the Devil's Plots

Julius T. Nganji

Our Warfare: Three Thrilling Plays to Uncover the Devil's Plots

Copyright © 2022 Julius T. Nganji

Published by Nganji Publishing
Gatineau (QC), Canada

Nganji.com

Illustrations: Sikutskido

ISBN: 9798847436281 (Paperback)

Library and Archives Canada Legal Deposit: 2022

For all persecuted Christians
who pass through tough times, trials, and temptations,
but keep their eyes fixed on Jesus Christ.

ACKNOWLEDGEMENTS

I would like to acknowledge all those who in one way or another, contributed to the success of this work. Many thanks to all those who encouraged me in play writing.

Thanks to Pastor Ambola David whose request led to the writing of *Just a Bit of Alcohol*. I also thank Mizpah C.B.Y.F; the youth wing of Mizpah Baptist Church, Limbe in Cameroon for ministering to people using these plays.

My older brother Edwin Nganji's love for plays and film acting has been a great encouragement. Keep up big brother!

Above all, I give all thanks and glory to God Almighty for the inspiration, strength, saving and sustaining grace.

TABLE OF CONTENTS

ACKNOWLEDGEMENTS iv

PREFACE ix

SAVIOUR AND LORD? 1

    CHARACTERS...2

    ACT ONE SCENE ONE..2

    ACT ONE SCENE TWO 3

    ACT TWO SCENE ONE 5

    ACT TWO SCENE TWO 7

    ACT THREE SCENE ONE 9

JUST A BIT OF ALCOHOL 11

    CHARACTERS...12

    PROLOGUE 12

    ACT ONE SCENE ONE..14

    ACT ONE SCENE TWO 17

    ACT ONE SCENE THREE 20

    ACT ONE SCENE FOUR 21

    ACT TWO SCENE ONE 22

    ACT TWO SCENE TWO 25

    ACT TWO SCENE THREE 27

    ACT THREE SCENE ONE 27

    ACT THREE SCENE TWO 29

    ACT THREE SCENE THREE 32

THE FALL OF THE TEMPLE PROSTITUTE 33

CHARACTERS 34

PROLOGUE 34

ACT ONE SCENE ONE 36

ACT ONE SCENE TWO 39

ACT ONE SCENE THREE 40

ACT ONE SCENE FOUR 42

ACT TWO SCENE ONE 45

ACT TWO SCENE TWO 47

ACT TWO SCENE THREE 48

ACT TWO SCENE FOUR 49

ACT THREE SCENE ONE. 51

ACT THREE SCENE TWO 52

ACT THREE SCENE THREE 53

ACT THREE SCENE FOUR 54

ACT FOUR SCENE ONE 55

ACT FOUR SCENE TWO 55

EPILOGUE 56

PREFACE

It is scarce to find Christian plays and poems in bookstores and libraries today. This book is intended to present plays that Christian groups can act, to help fulfil the Great Commission.

It is my sincere desire that many will come to the saving knowledge of Jesus Christ through these three plays. ***Saviour and Lord?*** focuses on the need to make Jesus Christ the Lord of our lives, ***Just A Bit of Alcohol*** was written in a context where alcohol was problematic and had disrupted some families, thus the need to discourage consumption in such circumstances. ***The Fall of The Temple Prostitute*** reveals God's sovereign power to deliver His church from the powers of darkness, making them more than conquerors.

Since most people prefer films these days, these plays could also be acted as films to reach a wider audience, exposing more people to the gospel.

x

SAVIOUR AND LORD?

Christ is not only interested in saving us from sin and its consequences but in fellowshipping with us in an intimate and personal relationship. He wants to be the Lord of our lives, empowering and directing us; so that we can daily live victorious Christian lives. This is possible only when we surrender all to his Lordship. He wants to be a part of our daily lives.

"Behold, I stand at the door and knock. If anyone hears my voice and opens the door, I will come in to him and eat with him, and he with me." (Rev. 3:20).

CHARACTERS

1. Kani
2. Bimi
3. Jesus Christ (Invisible)

ACT ONE SCENE ONE

(The place is a living room, well furnished with expensive decorative items to portray a rich man's living room. Kani is counting some money from his suitcase. He recalls past glories, with an optimistic view of the future. He expects life to end when he is old and tired of it. While counting the money, he unexpectedly hears a knock at the door and hurries up to stack the money which he then hides and rushes to open the door).

Kani: Four, five million, … *(pause)*. Who is that coming to disturb me? Kock, kock, kock *(mockingly)*. That is how they always knock. Don't be surprised to hear him begging for money with the usual many lazy complaints.

(Pauses for a minute and then answers as if he were happy, putting on a rather timid smile).

A minute please and I will be right there to let you in if you wish.

(He rushes to the door and opens it. He is surprised at the strange face he sees).

Who is this stranger arrayed in a golden apparel like a heavenly messenger? Do you think I could be of any help to you?

(Listens attentively, then replies).

Really? You mean you are Jesus Christ the son of God? *(listens).* Saviour of the world? That is interesting but what do you really want here?

(Pauses and shakes his head for a while and then ponders over the words he hears. He puts his hands into his pockets and walks away from the door as if strolling. He comes back shortly. He is proud being rich).

So, you say you want to be Saviour and Lord of my life? *(Laughs).* It is interesting *(pause).* You know I have always been a master and a saviour to many. So, you want me to bow before you? *(pause).*

Please, let me have some time in private to ponder over what you have said. I'll be right back.

ACT ONE SCENE TWO

(A young lady is seen in her room, putting on some seductive dress. She has a mirror and a lipstick with which she paints her lips while looking at the mirror and smiling. She is waiting for Kani- her unofficial boyfriend).

Bimi: Surely if Kani were around, he would have commended my designer dress. Wow, I am gorgeous. Listen to what he would have said "wow Bimi, you are very gorgeous as always". And I would have replied: thanks, Kani, I am always gorgeous for you.

(She looks at her watch and is so surprised that Kani is not yet around. She just can't believe).

What is wrong with Kani today? By now, we should have been in the heart of the dancing. Some roasted beef ('suyas'), roasted fish and bottles of drinks would have been consumed. The music booming in that night club, acting as a stimulant.

Kani is never that type who deceives. He is always on time. Surely, someone has interrupted him on his way or paid him a surprise visit. But why should he keep me in the cold? I need the warmth of his presence. I am still expecting him, but for how long?

(She hears a knock at the door and smiles hopefully. She greatly expects Kani).

It is surely Kani, I know he will never keep me in the cold. I told you he is not that type *(pause)*. Just a minute darling and I will be right there to let you in.

(She moves to the door and opens it expectantly).

Welcome Kan… *(Does not complete the pronunciation when she is caught by surprise)*. No, it isn't Kani. Who is this? *(long pause)*. Jesus Christ? Welcome. May I help you? *(Pauses and listens).* You mean you want to be Saviour and Lord of my life?

(Pauses and listens). That you came into the world and died for my sins? It's serious. A minute please let me consider your words.

ACT TWO SCENE ONE

(Kani, in his living room, pondering over Jesus' words. He does this loudly. Occasionally, he sits down, stands, and moves around).

Kani: Jesus Christ, Saviour of the world. Ah Christians are His followers, and they say He is from Heaven. But why has He brought Himself so low? What meekness! A president in this world would not even dine with a leper. If I were in His position, I would…

(Pockets his hands and moves around proudly, lifting his shoulders in pride as if he wanted them to grow taller than his head. He laughs for a while and then pauses to speak).

But His followers say anyone who *(raises his shoulders again with his hands in his pockets),* will be *(puts them down suddenly).*

That seems to be true because the shoulders will never grow taller than the head. Even Lucifer's couldn't. Ah! I almost forgot I was here for something. Oh! Jesus' words to me. *(Recalls them slowly, counting his fingers).*

"Saviour of your life". Who would like to go to hell; a foolish man isn't he? Even the Old Serpent envies heaven. No objection to that. He can be Saviour of my life.

"Lord of your life". That seems to give a position of authority to the title holder. This certainly means He will have to control my entire budget, my cars, houses, businesses, everything.

Then since they say He is Holy, He will prevent me from going out with Bimi, the fairest amongst all women. He will ask me to cling to the miserable and dirty Mahshi; the so-called housewife who is not as attractive any longer.

Then, the many bottles of beer I consume daily. No, no I won't accept that. He may go away if He wouldn't accept to be Saviour and me, the unquestionable boss of my life who is accountable to none *(pauses and recalls)*.

Oh! He is still waiting for me outside. What patience He has, indeed as Patience *(Lifts up his hands and head looking up to the sky)*. Generous God, please give me some of His patience. *(Runs to the door)*.

Sir, I am very sorry for having kept you waiting this while *(pause)*. In a meeting with my thoughts, the following resolutions were made and sealed with a golden seal that cannot be broken by whosoever:

1. That you can be the Saviour of my life if you will take me to heaven.
2. The truth is more bitter than Quinimax, so I must vomit it now. That you cannot be the Lord of my life.

This has been signed by my memory that recorded the minutes as Secretary and my proud self, the master. *(Pauses and listens for a while).*

You mean you wouldn't accept that one? You should be very lucky and grateful to have half of my life. At least it's 50:50. *(Pause).* But I don't understand you sir, are you really going away? Well, see you when I will be 75 and approaching the grave.

ACT TWO SCENE TWO

(Bimi in her room making her own decision).

Bimi: But how can this be? Saviour and Lord? Where then will I place Kani? *(ponders).* Saviour is acceptable. Kani isn't my Saviour and none in the world can set me free from sin.

Lord? Kani is not my lord. I am neither a slave to him nor a house help. But if I give Him these positions, will He not keep me away from Kani the so-called sugar daddy?

Well, these are temporal things. At death, they all stay behind, and we carry our naked souls to stand like criminals to be judged by Him who is standing outside. His Spirit has always convicted me of sin, but I have been stubborn. Surely, this is a golden opportunity to be set free.

But the pleasures of this world are so attractive. Well, all are like the glory of the flowers. I remember His followers say this world will pass away.

(She starts singing)

"I'd rather live in that bright city, than to own earth's silver and gold

I'd rather have Jesus my Saviour, than the diamonds of a palace to hold

I'd rather live in a little shack by the road

Than here to own all earth's treasures, with no title to a future abode"

(She then runs to the door to meet Christ).

I am very sorry for having kept you waiting so long. Well, I have decided as follows:
1. That you should be the Saviour of my life.
2. That you should be the Lord of my life.

In addition, please forgive all my sins. Come into my life and stay with me. Please, help me forsake all the bad things I have been doing. Welcome Saviour and Lord.

Satan, I have no links with you. I command you to pack out your entire luggage and go away from my life never to return in Jesus' name. I am now married to Jesus Christ, so leave me alone!

(She shuts the door, comes in and asks Christ to take the chair she was sitting on).

Sit thou here Lord and be thou exalted. What would you that I do? Where would you that I go? Speak Lord for your servant is ready to obey.

ACT THREE SCENE ONE

(Bimi and Kani are seen in two different places. Bimi is in great enjoyment while Kani is in terrible suffering. He laments his doom).

Kani: But I don't understand. Where am I? I now remember *(pause)*. Sad, sad story to tell. I was driving in my limousine two weeks after Jesus Christ visited me and I rejected Him; going to meet Bimi. Suddenly, a reckless truck driver sent me into a river. If I could get hold of him, then I would squeeze out his tiny bowels for depriving me of sweet life on earth.

(He surprisingly sees Bimi on the other side in enjoyment).

Oh, my goodness! Is that not Bimi enjoying herself over there while I am in torments? Are my eyes failing me? Is that not Jesus Christ with her?

(He curves his hands around his mouth and calls on her while waving his hands).

Hey! Hey! Bimi! It's me Kani, yes, I am in torments. How did you find yourself there when you were not up to my standard on earth? This is not fair!

Bimi: I received Jesus Christ on the day you deceived me we had an appointment. He transformed my life and forgave all my sins. He made me His child when I accepted Him as Saviour and Lord of my life. I drove away the devil, breaking all links between us.

Kani: Wait! Wait! You mean you let Him be the Saviour and Lord of your life, not Saviour only? *(pause)*. Oh! I wanted Him to be Saviour of my life only and not Lord.

Bimi: Yes, I did. It costed me nothing to accept Him; but all to follow Him. After calling me home from that sinful world, He has richly rewarded me as you can see. I am free, free, free from all sins, sickness, and sorrow.

Kani: Oh! No, had I known. I would have made Him Saviour and Lord of my life. Please Jesus, I will let you have these positions. I am no longer the boss of my life *(listens)*. That it is too late? Ok, just this favour please. Let Bimi dip her finger in water and cool my tongue for I am tormented in these flames.

No way? Oh! Christ, I rebelled against you. I strove for the world's wealth and pleasures. You are just, there is no partiality in you. How could I have denied my Creator? I must have been insane.

Your word is fulfilled this day. Truly, **"what does it profit a man to gain the whole world and forfeit his soul?"**.

THE END

JUST A BIT OF ALCOHOL

God's desire for us is to live a daily abundant and victorious Christian life, empowered and directed by the Holy Spirit. He therefore commands us to be filled with the Holy Spirit rather than with wine and other things that distract us from him. When the Holy Spirit comes into us, He gives us boldness and equips us for service, sealing and preserving us.

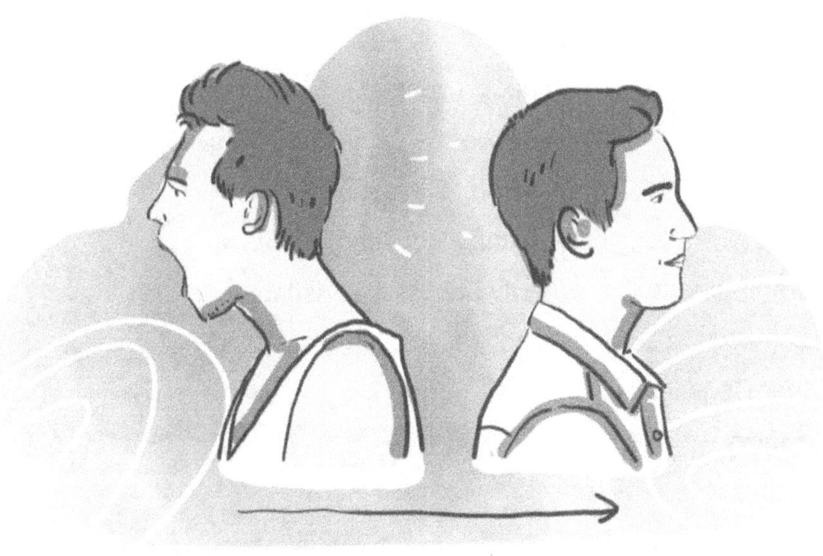

"Wine is a mocker, strong drink a brawler, and whoever is led astray by it is not wise". (Prov. 20:1)

CHARACTERS

Soung Wo……..	The Pastor
Mola Lyonga…..	A Deacon
Chika…………..	A Deaconess
Ngwa………….	A Deacon
Essomba………	A Deacon
Tata……………	A pagan and traditionalist
Kenfack………..	A pagan
Ma Adamu…….	A backslidden Christian, converted from Islam
Mrs Lyonga……	A desperate Christian
Besingi…………	A faithful Christian
Ngole…………..	A faithful Christian
Sarah Mbango…	Newly baptised Christian
Ikechukwu……..	Deaconess Chika's husband
Other Christians	
Villagers	
Pastor's wife	
Sarah's parents	

PROLOGUE

(All actors, one after another pass on the stage, each performing an act to draw the audience's attention. Christians

and pagans, inhabitants of the land of Mruh expose what they are. Pastor Soung Wo has a big Bible, preaching against alcoholism. Deacon Lyonga and Deaconess Chika each have bottles of alcohol. Other people holding bottles of various alcoholic beverages and drinking from these, flank Deacon Lyonga. Each misbehaves on stage due to the influence of the alcohol).

Soung Wo: Woe! Woe to you heroes of the wine bottle whose interests are not in the spiritual growth of God's people but to mislead them in alcoholism.

(Exit)

Mola Lyonga: Who says a deacon should not drink alcohol? *(Laughs and staggers drunkenly).* At least, for the stomach's sake and wisdom, not forgetting boldness to climb on the necks of those so-called born-again people in our church.

(Exeunt)

Chika: Long live chief deacon, deaconess Chika, iron lady *(laughs while drinking from her beer (33 Export) bottle. She is dressed in a white robe as from a communion service).*

So, Pastor Soung Wo thinks he has prevented me from taking alcohol today; even if he refuses to drop a little in the communion cup, I'll use this to mix it well.

After all, the reaction would be felt only within me. My body will not cry again for lack of alcohol *(laughs).* They can't see me now; I can drink as I desire. Then since I am beautiful, I will sleep with all the men in this village *(laughs and staggers drunkenly).*

(Exit).

ACT ONE SCENE ONE

(The place is a newly baptised Christian's home where the church leaders and deacons are feasting. They have just finished eating and drinks are being served. Some of the deacons ask for alcohol as they drink, while taking their turns to advice the candidate).

Mola Lyonga: Brothers and sisters in Christ, we thank God so much for our child and sister in Christ Sarah Mbango who has just accepted Christ into her life. Surely, the great leaders of our church will have some words of advice and encouragement to her and her family. Let them take their rounds in doing that, after which Pastor Soung Wo will conclude as we go to the next candidate's home.

Essomba: Thank you very much Mola Lyonga. People of God, it gives me great joy to advice this baby Christian. I thank God that I have been a Christian for 35 years and have never seen this age-old tradition die. I am only afraid of the young ones coming up; they are unable to uphold it. How would the world know that one is a Christian if we don't do this?

Sarah, Jesus Christ is powerful and able to help you always. Never fail to study the Bible and pray. Always attend church services and be kind to all people you meet, and God will bless you. Thank you all for the chance to speak. *(Sits down and continues to drink).*

(Ngwa rises with a bottle of beer (33 Export) in his hand. He speaks and pauses to drink while half drunk).

Ngwa: Papa and Mama to Sarah. Thank you all for this great reception. *(Points at them).* Have you seen the example your daughter is setting? You must repent, or you'll perish. It makes no sense to sit at home on Sundays, belonging to a juju society. At least, be a member of our church even if you still belong to the society. Who knows, Jesus Christ might have mercy on you because you are enrolled in His church.

(Drunken) Sarah, Sarah let me never hear that you have joined those born-again people in our church in going out to preach. Chei! Since when did our denomination start going out to preach? And they even say it is bad to take alcohol. What a disgrace to our church! Is that the message Alfred Saker and Joseph Merrick brought? No! else they would not have succeeded.

This is our culture; we socialise by taking alcohol. So, well *(pauses and thinks, then staggers drunkenly)* no one is perfect. Before I take my seat, try as much as you can to do all what we tell you and not all what we do. *(Sits down).*

Chika: My beloved sister, God will bless you and your parents this day *(drunken).* I know Sango is eager to speak, but I must finish what I have. The wine is getting sweeter now. Let us sing this song as I continue, *"Let us go into Canaan, we shall see*

Jesus our Lord, He is there turning water into wine, let us go, let us go".

We are Africans. We cannot ignore our ancestors and gods even when we worship God. This is an achievement, and we must acknowledge them for it. Let us rise as we pour a bit of this wine to them. *(Some rise while others do not. The pastor rushes to stop her but the act is already done).*

Pastor Soung Wo: Abomination, stop! Stop! *(surprised).* When did we start doing this? You even mentioned Saker and Merrick; is this what they taught us? Have you forgotten that God Almighty says we should have no other god but Him? Why invite God's wrath on yourselves?

Woe, woe unto those who mislead others. See how drunk you all are. You always say *'just a little alcohol for the stomach'* and end up in excess, excess that showers disgrace. See how you have disgraced the body of Christ. Can you now justify the taking of a bit of alcohol? Rise up let us leave. *(To hosts now)* Thank you all for your reception; but we can't continue.

Ngwa: You can go alone Sango, perfect man *(Spits).* I spit on those who despise ceremonies offered by others for the sake of alcohol. We will not leave this place unless the wine dries off the containers.

(Pastor angrily leaves as they continue to drink for some time. They all leave, drunk and cursing one another; some crying).

ACT ONE SCENE TWO

(At the assembly of Christians. Chika presides).

Chika: If there is no other point under the matters arising from the previous minutes, let us go on to New Matters *(Pause)*. The Pastor has something to say. You have the floor, man of God.

Pastor: Thank you very much sister Chika, chairperson of our church *(Pause)*. I was very shocked by the behaviour of some of our leaders last Sunday after the baptism. It would appear all the messages on alcoholism and drunkenness have been falling on deaf ears.

Lyonga*: (Chuckles).* Aha! I knew that would be the point you'll raise today. Why not call out our names and come out clearly; why remain as cunning as the serpent?

Essomba: So, Sango Pastor, do you blame us for drinking alcohol?

Pastor: I blame you all for hating the weaker brethren to the extent of getting drunk and disgracing our church. You've always said it is not bad to drink a bit of alcohol. But see how you always disgrace us while tasting it.

We ought to learn from the mistakes of people like Lot and Noah and not stumble. This is the fifth occasion. The Bible says, *'wine is a mocker, strong drink a brawler, and whoever is led astray by it is not wise'.* If you are not wise, you are a fool *(pause).*

It is time our church takes its stand against alcoholism. I think discipline should be strictly implemented on all the victims for persisting in alcoholism.

(Deaconess Chika rises in anger to address him).

Chika: Discipline who? Who disciplines who? Is it the employer or the employee? Members of our church, can Sango prove to us that it is bad to take alcohol? If he can, then we would accept discipline.

Look Sango, we employed you into this church and have the right to suspend your salary or send you away *(pause)*. Is it your business when we get drunk? Yours is to preach the Bible, upholding and protecting the age-old doctrines of our denomination.

Do you not know that only a foolish man urinates in the river that quenches his thirst? If you take any further step, you'll soon leave this church. After all, there are many pastors outside waiting to fill any vacancy in this prestigious church of ours.

Mola Lyonga: Sango, I know you are a pastor, but you are just as old as my last son. Let me advice you. *(Clears his throat by coughing)*. Many pastors have pleaded with us and even seen me personally to negotiate for a place here.

What experience do you have that could be compared with those who have been in the field for 30 years? They have been drinking alcohol and encourage their Christians to take a bit of it.

You are still fresh in the field and have much to lose if you are expelled. I only pity your wife and the children she will bear if this happens to you. Sit quiet and let us do what we want.

Pastor: How the devil takes his throne right amid God's people. I will never compromise my stand against alcoholism. I am not in the field for the sake of money.

Thank God that we ought not to live by bread alone. My God will not forsake me to the point of begging for bread. By God's grace, I will fight against it even to the point of shedding my blood.

I don't care, you can send me away from this church or other churches; but the message must be preached. I will take it all over our denomination.

Chika: O.K. We are already out of time. I'll like all members of the Board of Deacons to meet on Friday at 5:00 p.m. prompt so we can take a decision that will suit the church. The Pastor's presence is not needed in that meeting. You can close us with a word of prayer.

Pastor: Thank you father for such a time as this when your word would be preached, and your name exalted. We have sinned against you. Please, forgive us. Deliver us oh Lord from the power of strong drinks in Jesus' name. Amen.

(Exeunt)

ACT ONE SCENE THREE

(Board of Deacons meeting in an inner chamber in the church)

Chika: I thank you all brethren for being on time today. You are all aware of the fact that we must oust Sango from our midst, or he'll expose us.

Lyonga: That's true. He has always opposed us. It is time we send him away or he'll incite people against us. Besides, he might discover the mismanagement of funds.

Essomba: My heart has not been at peace. Ever since you started discussing this issue, there has been a Supreme Court meeting within me. I feel many Judges condemning me.

Sango is God's anointed, and God warns us not to touch or harm him. Let him go on, if the message he preaches is not from God, it will soon die. Remember we are church leaders; our lives are like cities on hills. Many people copy from us.

I can hear a voice judging me. *"Woe, woe if you mislead one of these little ones".* Another shouting *"it would be better if you were not born";* then a third voice *"a stone will be tied around your neck and thrown into the sea. Take your stand now against that alcoholism".* Brethren, we must not go that way.

Ngwa: What makes you think it is God and not your selfish motives speaking to you? Since when has God been speaking to our generation? Those things ceased many years ago. Well, we are a democratic denomination and I suggest Mrs. Chairperson that we vote on this matter now.

Chika: That's right. We ought to hit the iron while it is still very hot. Let me see those who are in favour of our decision. Please indicate by a hand show. *(All except Essomba put up their hands).*

(Exeunt)

ACT ONE SCENE FOUR

(The pastor in his house, with his wife praying for the church and village).

Pastor: Beloved wife, thanks be to God Almighty for helping us to rise this day to glorify Him. Let us continue to pray for God's guidance and direction for our church.

Pastor's Wife: Father, you will not let your people perish. Oh God, kindly deliver the church from alcoholism, the tricks, and plots of our enemy the devil. Please Lord, remove the scales from their eyes. Kindly cleanse your church from alcoholism and strong drinks in Jesus' name.

Pastor: Yes Lord, it is your deliverance we need. Also sustain your servant and his family, so that men will understand that you care for your own. Be ever exalted in Jesus' name we pray. Amen.

Pastor's wife: Amen.

Pastor: Beloved, let me take a bath and rush out to share the gospel this day. We must keep up the fight against excessive alcoholism in his village and in Jesus' name, we shall prevail.

(Exeunt).

ACT TWO SCENE ONE

(At a drinking spot, some villagers sit drinking. There are various local well fermented alcoholic drinks: mbuh, matango, raffia wine, shaa, afofo etc).

Tata: Chei! Those Christians are hypocrites. Do you know some always hiddenly join us here in drinking but claim not to do so when they are in their church?

Kenfack: Really? I know they ought not to drink alcohol if they would be effective in serving their God. Normally, when I fill my stomach with wine, I hardly reason or make good judgments. The excitement within prevents me from working.

Ma Adamu: In Islam, we were not allowed to take alcohol. To us, it is the devil's property. I am sorry to tell you that I have backslidden from it just because I was converted to Christianity and discouraged by their leaders. I like Christianity because it is real. Their God is real and powerful. I only need encouragement to be effective.

Mola Lyonga: If you don't know anything about our church, keep quiet. Yes, we have dismissed our pastor because of foreign doctrine and beliefs. His claims are not biblically founded. There is no portion of the Bible that says we should not drink alcohol.

Tata: I don't know your Bible well Lyonga. I am a traditionalist, upholding our tradition. But I don't know if your Bible also says you should drink alcohol.

Lyonga: Of course, but I cannot readily quote that passage. We are advised to take a little for our stomachs.

Kenfack: *(laughs mockingly).* Aha! For the sake of the stomach, you say and just a little. That makes me think it is a medication for a specific illness. You are always drinking here, does that mean you always have problems with your stomach? Leave wine to some of us who are perishing as some of your faithful brothers say.

Ma Adamu: Kenfack is right. When I was converted to Christianity, I was told that the Bible says it is not for kings to drink wine. Not only are pastors kings, but ordinary Christians as well. What more of Deacons or Elders?

Lyonga: I have clearly understood your arguments. You all are right. But you see; I am always very straight forward in the way I do my things. How will they expect me to eliminate alcohol when I am still living in this community? How would you all feel when I organise a ceremony and only serve sweet drinks as some of them preach? At least, I should please everyone who comes.

Tata: You are right Mola Lyonga. I told you I am a traditionalist, deeply rooted. I am a member of the most secret juju cult in the palace. I know that one must be completely on one side to be effective.

There should be no sitting on the fence. That is why I don't even go to church. Your pastor is right, he does not take pleasure in the things we do.

To us, alcohol is good, and I can take as much as I desire. My advice to you is that you either stand fully as a Christian or you join us.

Kenfack: *(laughs)*. Wisdom, wisdom. Indeed, there is wisdom in the cup, wisdom undiluted. Not just any cup but that which is well fermented for tough men.

My wife and children are Christians. I am the only one out of Christianity, the white man's religion *(pause)*. I am a Bamileke man, you all know. We love our tradition. There is one thing that surprises me about my wife and children. Despite all the beatings and so-called persecutions, they are still firm. They have never lacked even when I don't provide for them.

I have always used alcoholism as a means of forgetting the problems I face, seeing them as Christians. Of course, it has helped. When I get drunk, I am merry and forget about my problems for the period. It is also a means of socialising. At least a man must take it to be brave. The church would be doing wrong to completely stop it.

Tata: You are right Kenfack *(pause)*. We are glad to have Deacon Lyonga in our company today. We would appreciate you paying our bills from your refreshment allowance *(laughs)*.

Lyonga: It has been a pleasure being with you all. You see, I don't play the hypocrite; that is why I drink openly and give to those who want it. I don't speak against it and drink behind as some do. But I don't encourage my children to take it, because of its negative effects *(pause)*.

Ma Adamu, come and collect your money. Let me leave now, tomorrow is Sunday.

ACT TWO SCENE TWO

(The place is the Pastor's house. He is praying with his family and some caring Christians).

Pastor: Thank you all brethren for this encouraging visit. I would like us to commit our church leaders to God in prayers as we plead for God's forgiveness and ask Him to deliver them.

Ngole: Father, our God. We plead that your mercy and not your wrath be upon our church leaders. Have mercy on them for having given themselves to alcoholism and the love of money, for having led your children astray.

(As they are praying, Mrs. Lyonga suddenly enters the house crying as they stop to listen to her).

Mrs Lyonga: Oh pastor, I am doomed. I thought it was a right decision to send you out of our church but never foresaw what would happen.

Lyonga returned late at about 1:00 a.m. already drunk. He had me well beaten after I refused him food for not giving me money to cook food. The spirit of alcoholism now controls the church.

Please, do not be angry with us, else God's wrath is upon us and our families for sending you His anointed away, and defiling His temple.

Pastor: Mrs. Lyonga, weep not. God is merciful to those who truly repent. I thank God you acknowledge that. We are here just for that purpose. Join us in praying for them.

Besingi: Father, kindly deliver your people from the spirit of alcoholism. Help them Lord, to see its ills in Jesus' name.

Pastor: As we pray, just confess your sins to God and repent of them. *(Pause).* Heavenly father, merciful God; you are God whose standards do not change with the changing world. You are Holy and just. You've commanded us to be holy as you are and to be filled with your Holy Spirit instead of wine.

I thank you for listening to us this day, forgiving our sins and healing our church. We desire to see you descend and purge our church. I believe you will do it oh Lord, in the name of Jesus Christ. Amen.

(Besingi and Ngole each present to the pastor's wife some food and money).

Besingi: Pastor, I thank God for your courage and firmness during times like this when man fails. Truly, it is better to trust in God than to have confidence in man. My family and I have only this token to present to you. Please, receive it.

Pastor: God bless you brother.

Ngole: Yes pastor, God's word is true. His people do not beg for bread. It is true that through birds, God fed Elijah. He clothes the lilies and feeds the birds.

God laid in my heart to support you with this token as you go around proclaiming His word and delivering people from the powers of strong drinks. If you had not preached against it, all my money would have been used in paying hospital bills after getting me out of gutters.

My home would have been scattered and my children desperate as I see with some friends who persist in alcoholism. Keep up man of God! God is with you. No one can destroy God's truth.

Pastor: I thank you all for obeying God's command to flee from sin. Thank you for being good examples. Continue to be strong in your service to Him, teaching others what He has taught you.

My lovely wife and I accept your wonderful gifts and pray God to bless you even ten folds in Jesus' name! Amen.

ACT TWO SCENE THREE

(The Pastor in his house praying for the church. He is kneeling).

Pastor: Heavenly Lord, I thank you for the opportunity to pray for our church. Kindly intervene Lord and help the villagers also believe in you as you purge your church in Jesus' name. Amen.

ACT THREE SCENE ONE

(Deaconess Chika's husband chasing her with a cutlass as people run after them to intervene).

Ikechukwu: Chika, I will slaughter you today! Did you come to another man's land to sleep with all the men in this village?

Chika: Help, help. Hold him please!

(Villagers gather as some hold Ikechukwu. Besingi and Ngole arrive).

Besingi: Ikechukwu! Ikechukwu stop! *(Holds him as he is breathless).* What is the matter Deaconess Chika?

Ikechukwu: This hypocrite of a deaconess; she has been cheating on me. Which normal woman will return home late in the night and smelling alcohol? That is not even the main thing. I caught her with Tata on my matrimonial bed. He had given her alcohol to the extent that she could accept all he said.

Can you imagine a member of the secret society lying with my wife? Abomination! I spit on women who are controlled by alcohol *(pause).* I know I am a foreigner, but God will do me justice. I will fight against this even to death. Where will I hide my head and throw away this disgrace? Which river can accept to swallow it?

Chika: It's a lie, it's a lie! He is just persecuting me!

Ikechukwu: I'll kill you hypocrite!

Ngole: Haba! Deaconess Chika. Do I not smell wine all over your body? Do you see the consequences of expelling a just man of God because he takes a stand against alcoholism? Repent oh! Repent or it will be terrible. See how you invite God's wrath on you. How you disgrace the church of God.

Where do you place the weaker brethren? Who knows, (pause) those we often call weaker brethren may even be stronger and more devoted than us.

Besingi: Forgiveness please I pray you. Forgiveness Ikechukwu. God is the Judge. Hold your peace please.

Ngole: I know it is difficult, but for Christ's sake, please forgive her.

(Ikechukwu throws his cutlass, turns his back and leaves while weeping, head downward. Besingi and Ngole leave as villagers gradually leave, abandoning Chika).

ACT THREE SCENE TWO

(A meeting of Christians. Members against the leaders; they request for Pastor Soung Wo to be reinstated).

Mrs Lyonga: We want pastor Soung Wo back to our church. He must come back, or you'll lead an empty church.

Ngole: Yes, that is what we want. We can't bear the disgrace in this village any longer. How many times will unbelievers sit to talk about our church? Even in beer houses! If we had newspapers in this village, we would be featured on all the cover pages.

The other day it was Lyonga beating his wife late in the night after getting drunk. Then most recently, Deaconess Chika; head of all deacons in our church caught in adultery that attracted the whole village. Oh God have mercy.

Essomba: It is time we take a stand as a church against alcoholism. You have been hiding behind the fact that it makes you bold. Has God not said that His Spirit will give us boldness when He comes into us? You say it is a way of socialising, can we not socialise without alcohol? You will also say it makes you forget your problems; do the problems not reappear when you are in your normal state?

Enough, enough of that. We must take a stand against this. You either repent of that or leave this church; we are not the ones to leave. There is no compromise about that. The church is not your property.

Besingi: Yes, pastor Soung Wo must come back to this church. We are the decision makers and not you leaders. You are there for us. You either take your stand against alcoholism or be flushed out.

Ngwa: *(repentant).* Brethren, I was a fool. Indeed, the Bible says he who is misled by alcohol is not wise and so he is a fool. Please forgive me for having disgraced you and the church. I stood against the pastor and voted for his dismissal. He was just. He is the right person here.

Some pastors take alcohol and even laugh at men who don't consume it, but our pastor is a good example to emulate. He is truly a man of God. Let him come back. Please forgive me. I repent.

Chika: *(weeping).* I have disgraced you and this church. I made myself a public toilet, sleeping with men in exchange for a bottle of alcohol. Please forgive me. In my alcoholism, I visited witchdoctors to maintain my position as chief deacon of our church.

I ordered God's money to be used as refreshment allowance after each meeting, just to take some alcohol. You are all just; you can discipline me. Please forgive me. I am not fit to be called a child of God, let alone a church leader.

Ngole: I thank you Holy God for convicting your people after a long period of resistance. Thank you for uncovering what has been covered for so many years. You are a faithful God. No one can play games with your word to suit him. You are God.

Lyonga: Who am I brethren to oppose the Holy Spirit? I took a way that seemed right but whose end was destruction. I thank God all merciful, for keeping me alive to repent.

I had used the scriptures to justify myself. I misinterpreted it to suit me. *"He who does not drink should not condemn he who drinks"* and *"take a little wine for your stomach"* were my best verses. I always felt uncomfortable when *"wine is a mocker"* was read. Lord, I join others to fight against alcoholism.

(To his wife) Please forgive me, forgive me. I was a fool. I was foolish.

Ngole: Well brethren, you have all heard and are witnesses. God has cleansed His church and appointed His servant. Let us go and prepare to receive His servant, Pastor Soung Wo, and his family. This village must hear the good news.

Our church in its by-laws must clearly state its stand and disciplinary actions against alcoholism, even right down to the families.

ACT THREE SCENE THREE

(In the church. Pastor Soung Wo and family welcomed. People are worshipping God with songs as some of the villagers run in. Tata surrenders to Christ).

Chika: Man of God, on behalf of the leaders of our church, I plead for your forgiveness. We were wrong in the way we treated you. Please forgive us. We have unanimously taken our stand against alcoholism and would join you to fight against it.

(Tata comes forward, removes his cap, cup, and bag as he surrenders them).

Tata: Truly, your God is great. I have decided to serve your God and not the gods of this land. What I have seen your God do is marvellous in my sight. Pastor Soung Wo is truly His servant. He stood firm even in starvation and still had energy to preach out against alcoholism.

Pastor: Praise the Lord! God is good all the time; all the time God is good. We must stand out against alcoholism and discourage it in all its forms. The Spirit of God will back us in our struggle against it in Jesus' name! Amen.

(A song; "Jesus is a winner man" is tuned as they sing and dance).

THE END

THE FALL OF THE TEMPLE PROSTITUTE

Christians are often involved in warfare with the devil, the accuser of our brethren. He always seeks their downfall. God nevertheless equips His children with an armour, to conquer the devil. He thus makes them more than conquerors! God says the battle is His.

"For we do not wrestle against flesh and blood, but against the rulers, against the authorities, against the cosmic powers over this present darkness, against the spiritual forces of evil in the heavenly places — For the weapons of our warfare are not of the flesh but have divine power to destroy strongholds" (Ephesians 6:12; II Cor. 10:4).

CHARACTERS

Kongnyu---------- The Pastor

Wepnyu---------- A Deacon

Akele-------------- A Christian

Menke------------ A Christian

Fake-------------- A Deaconess

Talla---------------- Fake's husband, a traditionalist

Cockhiary--------- Princess of the coast, the Temple Prostitute-
Mimi

Mallah------------ Queen of the coast

Ta Ngiri----------- Witchdoctor

Ake---------------- An Unbeliever

Itabih-------------- An Unbeliever

Voice

Narrator

PROLOGUE

(Mallah is seen sitting in her kingdom anxiously waiting for Cockhiary. She gets up and impatiently walks around for a while then sits down. She anxiously looks at her watch and then stands up to speak).

Mallah: What is wrong with Cockhiary, why has she not come back? And she has an important mission from the master.

(The Narrator fearfully moves towards her and then faces the audience to speak).

Narrator: The Christians are waxing strong. The evil one has found no way of pulling them down. He has however devised a new plan which he must experiment. Listen to this.

(Narrator moves aside to reveal Cockhiary who is already in. She prostrates herself before Mallah in respect. Mallah commissions her).

Cockhiary: Queen Mallah, here I am. I am very sorry for my lateness which is because I wanted to properly carry out my assignment.

Mallah: That is alright Princess Cockhiary, the most beautiful and seductive.

(She stands up, moves towards her and squats to touch her long hair while assigning her).

The master has conceived a new idea which he wants you to implement because of your experience in this field.

Cockhiary: I am at your service mama. What should I do to that stubborn church?

Mallah: Ever ready Princess Cockhiary. I love you my daughter *(pause)*. Deaconess Fake has been barren for fifteen years and is badly in need of a child. Ta Ngiri will be there to put you into her womb. You will be born after five months of pregnancy yet will be stronger than any other child; because of the substance you will be made of.

When you grow up, seduce the men in that church. Set the church into immorality and confusion. Their homes must not be at peace but in pieces (*pause*). Now listen to me; let me warn you. The Pastor must be your last focus because he is very powerful.

Cockhiary:(*Gets up, kneels, and swears to the queen*). I would do that. I swear (*rubs her finger on the ground and licks it to show sincerity, devotion, and seriousness*).

Mallah: Then be fast about it.

(*Mallah leaves as Cockhiary follows behind. Narrator comes back to his position, trembling*).

Narrator: Will they succeed? This will certainly depend on the prayer lives of those Christians. Let us see what happens.

(*Exit*)

ACT ONE SCENE ONE

(*Fake is discussing with her husband in their house. The talk is that of her barrenness*).

Talla: Ah Deaconess Fake, 'church woman'. Has your God not forsaken you? For fifteen years we have been together in what you call holy matrimony; yet without a child.

Fake: What do you want me to do? Is it not said that 'the patient dog eats the fattest bone?'

Talla: *(Hisses).* Ha-ah. Fattest bone after it has grown pale and its body wearing off? Of what use will the bone be to it when it will soon get into its grave? *(pause).* Look wife, you deceive yourself. I know that you would not like to consult Ta Ngiri about this.

Fake: My God forbids that.

Talla: Why then did you prefer me to those Christians when my words to you will be like water thrown on a cocoyam leaf?

Fake: I have hope that God will use me to set you free.

Talla: Am I bound by any chain? *(pause).* Well, that's not my interest. *(Pleading)* Fake, do not go with me to Ta Ngiri's temple. Only permit me go on your behalf.

Don't you see Labu and Iggi who were like yourself? They each have three children. Ta Ngiri helped them. *(Weeping)* Oh when I die who will inherit my property? Will my name not be wiped off the face of this earth?

Fake: *(Sympathetic).* Did you say I wouldn't go yet it would work?

Talla: Of course, I meant just what I said.

Fake: How can this be?

Talla: What is difficult with ordinary men is possible with Ta Ngiri. Only let me go on your behalf. Ta Ngiri will prepare the concoction which you will take. That's all; as simple as ABC.

Fake: No cutting of my body with a blade?

Talla: What for? That is for major cases. Yours is a minor case. Just speak the words.

(Queen of the coast appears to convince her as Fake bows her head to ponder over it. Mallah is invisible).

Mallah: Golden opportunity. Do you really need a child? Open your eyes and see. Other Christians have children except you. You have a curse in you that can only be broken by Ta Ngiri.

Order him to go on your behalf; this is the last chance you have. Opportunity comes once, don't miss this one.

Fake: Talla, you may go.

Talla: *(Claps and hugs her, demonstrating his joy).* That's good wife. You are fast moving towards maturity. That church and its religion was almost overwhelming you *(pause).* Now, do not attend Christian meeting today as you will have to take the concoction at 5:30 p.m.

Fake: Why shouldn't I; A Deaconess absent from church? Impossible.

Talla: O…..oh Fake; understand me. You must take the concoction at 5:30 p.m. and your meeting begins at 5:00 p.m. It would not be proper for you to start the meeting and then move out to take the medicine before going back to sit in the church.

Fake: It's alright then, go ahead and do as you wish but don't deceive me.

(Mallah rejoices and leaves. She goes ahead of Talla to Ta Ngiri's temple).

ACT ONE SCENE TWO

(There is a Christian meeting dedicated for prayers. The pastor gives out prayer points as the Christians pray).

Kongnyu: Beloved in the Lord, God revealed something to me last night which greatly burdens me.

(He is disturbed and pauses for a while. Christians are impatient and anxious to hear him speak).

Wepnyu: Man of God what is it all about?

Akele: We are eager to hear you speak. Please, tell us. We will bear it as our burden and pray for it.

Menke: Man of God, what is it that seals your mouth?

Kongnyu: My heart is indeed heavy *(pause).* It is choking me within. Yes, the forces of darkness are in operation amongst us. An agent has been sent to scatter our church.

Wepnyu: God forbid. Brethren let us pray so as not to fall into this trap. Let us be vigilant.

Akele: Yes, let us also pray for our brethren who are not here with us so that God might also protect them.

(They all pray on this topic, led by the pastor).

ACT ONE SCENE THREE

(Ta Ngiri is sitting on the floor of his temple meditating. Smoke rises out of a small pot as he speaks in a strange language to the audience. Mallah rushes in to inform him of Talla's arrival).

Mallah: Ngiri! Ngiri!

Ta Ngiri: *(Prostrates).* Welcome queen Mallah. What brings you here unexpectedly?

Mallah: Don't be troubled. You have something urgent to do. I am sorry I did not inform you of my coming. This is due to the urgency of the matter.

Talla and Fake have been in desperate need of a baby for fifteen years. Talla is on his way here for a concoction after a meeting with his wife. Take this *(she hands some concoction to him).*

Let him mix it with white honey and white powder. She should be instructed to drink nothing except palm wine until after delivery. She should expect the results after five months.

You may collect five francs from him. Here he comes, good luck and goodbye.

(Exit).

(Talla knocks at Ta Ngiri's door and is permitted to enter).

Talla: Is Ta Ngiri in; old one may I come in?

Ta Ngiri: Ha! Ha ! ha ! Welcome but enter as usual. No shoes and with your back. No laughter in here or crying. *(Lifts up his head and discovers it is Talla).* Ah, is it you Talla?

Talla: Yes, old one. I have come for…

Ta Ngiri: No! No! Don't tell me anything, I am not a kid witchdoctor *(pause).* I know you need a child.

Talla: That's right old one.

Ta Ngiri: Not only a child but children *(pause).* Your wife has been cursed without a child for fifteen years *(pause).* Yowah, yowah. I can do that. Only drop a five-franc coin into this pot.

(Talla removes the coin from his handkerchief and throws it into a small black pot filled with water).

Now call on your wife and tell her to receive her baby.

Talla: Fake! Fake! ….

(He hears his wife answering and is surprised).

Fake: Yes Talla, where are you darling what do you want?

Talla: Receive the baby!

Ta Ngiri: Good Talla! I will now give you this concoction. Wait a minute, let me bless it and make it lively. The child will confirm by answering. *(Invokes Cockhiary's spirit)* Cock! Cockhi! Cockhiary! Where are you? Help this desperate man!

Cockhiary: Here am I. I am coming!

Talla: *(Surprised).* Who is that what am I hearing?

Ta Ngiri: Don't be afraid *(laughs).* Take this and mix with white honey and white powder. Let her eat it every morning first thing when she gets up from bed; even before saying her morning prayers.

She must not drink anything except it is palm wine. *(Pauses and smiles confidently).* I give you five months, five months Talla to raise those cheeks that have fallen in disgrace for fifteen years.

Talla: You are all powerful old one. Thank you for solving my problem.

(Exit).

ACT ONE SCENE FOUR

(Fake is in the house preparing the table for her husband who is not yet back. Enter Talla swiftly as Fake finishes. He breathes tire fully).

Talla: Sweetheart! You must have been impatiently waiting for me.

Fake: *(Angry).* Is this 5:30 p.m? You have prevented me from attending my prayer meeting.

Talla: I'm sorry wife. Ta Ngiri delayed me. The case was not what I thought.

Fake: While you were away, I was resting on the bed when I heard you calling in a dream and asking me to receive the baby

(Pause). Well did you bring the concoction?

Talla: Dream? Did I hear you say dream?

Fake: Yes. Is anything wrong?

Talla: Well no. *(Pause).* I brought the concoction. I could not have come back empty handed. Ta Ngiri prepared it. Please bring some white powder, I have bought some white honey and palm wine for the concoction.

Fake: Palm what? Look Talla, don't play tricks on me. So now you want me to get drunk!

Talla: That is not the point. It is a requirement for the process. Besides, it is fresh and sweet palm wine; the type that is appropriate for women.

(She goes into the room and brings some white powder. Talla mixes the concoction and gives her after which he gives her a cup of the palm wine).

Bring out your left hand and receive it. Now lick it and expect a miracle within five months! Ta Ngiri says we should expect our son within this time.

(Mallah appears though invisible to both. She senses some stubbornness)

Fake: Why is it so nasty?

Mallah: *(Authoritatively).* Take it! Did you not send for it?

Talla: Eat it wife. Five months will come in the twinkling of an eye.

Fake: *(Licks it).* Quite bitter, though there is honey in it.

(Mallah rejoices and leaves).

Talla: *(Rejoices).* Good wife. I can now peacefully enjoy your delicious meal.

(He gets to the table and starts eating with much appetite).

Fake: I wish to sleep; I am feeling dizzy. Please, let me go and sleep.

Talla: *(Swallowing).* Go on wife, let me finish this delicious meal. I will join you later.

(The Narrator is so sad that he speaks with little courage).

Narrator: How their God grieves in times like this. Why should a Deaconess be the channel? Oh no! How the devil rejoices.

It is now five months since Deaconess Fake took the concoction. Fake has given birth to a charming baby girl. All is not well.

She has grown up to set the church into confusion. There is a terrible immorality and problems in homes. Her name is Mimi; no one knows her as Cockhiary except Mallah.

What next? Just watch!

ACT TWO SCENE ONE

(Ake and Itabi in a local palm wine bar discussing about Cockhiary and the latest happenings in the church.).

Ake: Itabi, I am glad I am not a Christian. Don't you see what is happening to that church?

Itabi: What is it again Ake?

Ake: Aha! Are you a stranger in this land? Haven't you heard about a Temple Prostitute that is troubling the church?

Itabi: Whose daughter, is she?

Ake: One of the elders of the church, Fake. Talla's wife.

Itabi: Talla the leader of the juju society in the palace?

Ake: You know that well. *(Pause).* The story goes that he agreed with his wife to consult Ta Ngiri for a child.

Itabi: *(Laughs):* A church leader accepted her husband to do that? This church has truly changed. When she just became a member, she detested all such things and never wanted to hear about them. Oh, time really changes people.

Ake: They call that daughter of hers Mimi. Her ways are terrible. I even dread her. She is very mischievous in her ways. Do you know that she has been going out with almost all the men in that church? Most of their homes are in confusion. Thank God my family is spared because we are not Christians.

Itabi: What is their pastor doing about it? It appears most of them are caught up in this mess.

Ake: I hear he has been having retreats upon retreats and praying about this.

Itabi: Foolishness! What prevents them from sending her away from their gathering?

Ake: Could it not be her supernatural power's influence over them? Who dares touch her or speak to her carelessly? I hear she even has charming eyes and an authoritative voice. Elders take to her instructions.

Itabi: Terrible! I hope this does not extend to our families. By the way I must evacuate my family out of this land before that witchcraft affects us.

Ake: *(laughs)* Man of little courage. Don't you understand? This cannot affect us. This is surely an agent on mission to the church to destroy it. Their activities have surely been affecting and disturbing them.

Itabi: Thank you brother but I must leave now. To be forewarned is to be forearmed.

(Exit)

Ake: *(Laughs).* What is the matter with our land? Men are becoming women!

ACT TWO SCENE TWO

(Cockhiary is in her room preparing to go out on her mission. Mallah appears to encourage her).

Cockhiary: *(Prostrates).* Welcome mama. Why are you here without any prior notification?

Mallah: My daughter, I have come to encourage and fortify you as you go out for your assignment today.

Cockhiary: Thanks mama for your care and concern.

Mallah: Go on and claim the victory. You have been working well. Entice the men by your dressing. Use this perfume to distract them.

You must always go to church services late and must put on shoes and dresses that will distract everyone *(Pause).* When you go, sit right in front, not too far from the pastor. Always remember to leave before they say their prayers.

Cockhiary: It's ok mama. *(Gets up).*

Mallah: *(Rubs her hands on Cockhiary's face).* I give you charming eyes to seduce the men and lure them to sleep.

Cockhiary: Thanks a million mama for this reinforcement.

Mallah: Goodluck and goodbye my daughter.

Cockhiary: Goodbye mama.

(Mallah exits).

Cockhiary: The husbands of Akele and Menke will be mine in a few months. I will make good use of my charming new eyes. *(pause)*

Deaconess Fake is now a mere churchgoer *(laughs)* thanks to Cockhiary. *(Pause)*. But that pastor is powerful, prayerful, and watchful. He shall be my last focus as mama instructed.

ACT TWO SCENE THREE

(The pastor is preaching as Mimi comes late. Many are distracted. Her mother is angry).

Pastor: *(Reads I Cor. 5:1)*. Brethren, it is with tears that I preach this day. There is a terrible immorality amongst us. Many have been blinded, enticed, and seduced.

(Cockhiary enters. All eyes on her except the Pastor who continues to preach. Cockhiary gets right in front and sits. She sits just in front of her mother).

Fake: What is wrong with you Mimi, why have you come so late?

Mimi: Mum I had to change my dress as on my way, a car splashed dirty water on me.

Pastor: *(Continues preaching as he now reads from I Cor. 6:9)*. Do you not know that your bodies are God's temple? *(Reads I Cor. 6:15)*. Many are caught up in immorality.

(Mimi looks at Wepnyu to seduce him. He gets up and tries to move towards her but realises himself and shamefully sits down. All are surprised).

Pastor: Brethren be prayerful so as not to fall into this temptation. God has equipped you with the power to resist.

(Mimi gets up and leaves. All eyes on her. Christians pray and leave as Wepnyu meets the pastor to complain to him).

Wepnyu: Pastor, I don't just understand what went wrong with me. I fell in deep instantaneous love with Mimi while you were preaching. I became confused when she looked at me and was almost attracted towards her. I felt a force lifting me off my seat.

Pastor: Brother, do not faint in prayers. The evil one is around. Let us get into prayer and fasting until God reveals it to us.

Wepnyu: May God help us in Jesus' name!

Pastor: Amen, He will surely do that.

(Exeunt)

ACT TWO SCENE FOUR

(The pastor is sitting in his house reading his Bible as Akele runs in crying. The pastor rises in fright).

Pastor: Wait woman! Sister Akele, what brings you here at this hour?

Akele: Pastor, my husband. He is not himself. He almost killed me yesterday. He says I have a demon.

Pastor: Your husband did?

Akele: Yes pastor. Today I saw him with sister Mimi. She came right into our home, prepared food and ate with my husband. As if that was not enough, they slept on our matrimonial bed.

Pastor: Oh, my goodness! Can this be the temple prostitute?

Akele: He packed out my things and sent me away with all our children. Mimi told him she had a vision that I am possessed and that there is a curse on the children. *(Pauses and sobs).*

My husband no longer reads the Bible neither does he pray. He now smokes and gets drunk.

(Menke swiftly enters and falls at the Pastor's feet, crying).

Pastor: *(Lifting her up).* What is wrong? Is it also Mimi?

Menke: As if you knew Pastor. There has been no peace in the house since she started visiting us. My husband turns down the food I prepare. He calls me a hag and praises Sister Mimi for her beauty.

Pastor: Never mind. I will seek God's face more about this. Our church is at the verge of collapse. *(Pause).* Now go home Menke and you Akele to your sister's home and spend the night.

I will see what I can do about it while waiting on God's supernatural intervention.

ACT THREE SCENE ONE.

(The Pastor meets with Wepnyu in his house for prayers. He reads from Ephesians 6:10-20. They pray about the situation of the church).

Pastor: Let us pray that God might reveal to us what is wrong with our church.

Wepnyu: Father we ask that you reveal to us the problem with our church. Why these problems Lord? Why this lukewarmness?

Pastor: Lord God, kindly reveal again clearly if this is what you had shown me. Let the eyes of our understanding be enlightened in Jesus' name. Oh God, church leaders are caught up in this mess. Arise oh Lord God and express your mighty power in Jesus' name we pray. Amen.

Wepnyu: Amen.

Pastor: Let us continue to trust God. As you go home, continue to pray.

(Wepnyu leaves. The Pastor gets to bed. After some few minutes of sleep, he starts dreaming. He wrestles with Cockhiary in his dream. He rolls on the bed while shouting).

Pastor: Is it you Mimi who wants to divide the church of God? (Pause). Would you come against me with charms? OK we will battle it out. (Pause). In Jesus' name!

(He wrestles for some time and then remains calm as he hears a voice speaking to him).

Why run again? I thought you claimed to be all powerful.

Voice: Kongnyu! Kongnyu! My son. Be not afraid, I have conquered your foe. Mimi is a demon; she is not a true human. She is the temple prostitute. She is on mission to the church.

She has been sent by Mallah the queen of the coast; to seduce men and cause immorality to reign in the church. She must cause people to hate holiness. Her real name is Cockhiary! Cockhiary!

(Pastor suddenly gets up and realises he was dreaming. He picks up a piece of paper and writes the dream).

Pastor: *(On his knees praying)* Thank you father for the revelation. I now understand why Akele and Menke came crying to me. Kindly bring the final victory in Jesus' name.

ACT THREE SCENE TWO

(Cockhiary is seen in her room trying to cure the parts of her body that have been wounded. She wipes it with cotton immersed in alcohol).

Cockhiary: Oh, why did I try him? That pastor is powerful indeed. He wounded all my body *(angry)*. I must revenge. I must get rid of his life!

(Mallah suddenly appears).

Mallah: Cockhiary! Cockhiary! Do not go. There is danger. Your plans have been uncovered. Return to the kingdom. At least you have done your best.

Cockhiary: Return without having finished my assignment? How can a mere Pastor challenge one with cosmic powers like me. I must go to that church tomorrow and kill him.

Mallah: No don't go, come back. Do not go and disgrace me.

Cockhiary: *(Crying).* No mama, I must go. A Spartan would never surrender.

Mallah: Go then; but remember the consequences if you disgrace me.

ACT THREE SCENE THREE

(The Pastor and Wepnyu are in the Pastor's house).

Pastor: Brother, God is faithful. After our meeting, He revealed the truth to me.

Wepnyu: He is indeed faithful. Do you know He revealed to me it is Mimi causing all the turmoil in this church? I wrestled with her in my dream; but God wrought the victory.

Pastor: God spoke clearly to me. He said Mimi is a demon on mission to our church. Her real name is Cockhiary and she is from the sea. She has been sent by Mallah; the queen of the coast to seduce Christians and cause immorality to reign in our church.

Wepnyu: Then let us pray that God may deliver our church from her hands.

Pastor: Father, we thank you for the victory. We are more than conquerors. Father, we ask that you bring deliverance to your church in Jesus' name.

Wepnyu: Also restore your children into the fellowship. We pray for Fake, Akele and Menke. We ask that your peace might reign in their homes in Jesus' name we have prayed. Amen.

Pastor: Amen.

(Exeunt).

ACT THREE SCENE FOUR

(The Christians are seriously praying as Cockhiary enters and sits behind. She gets up and tries to charm the pastor but falls at the mention of the name of Jesus Christ).

Pastor: In the name of Jesus Christ, we arrest all demonic forces present in this place.

(Cockhiary falls and starts trembling. Christians open their eyes as many of them are afraid. Deaconess Fake is not present in this meeting).

Akele: Pastor come, pastor. Look at her eyes.

Menke: Yes pastor, she moves like a snake. Help pastor.

(The pastor and Wepnyu come forward and pray for her).

Wepnyu: In the name of Jesus, spirit of the coast, come out of her.

(She trembles increasingly).

Pastor: Cockhiary spirit, come out. We command you to pack out your luggage and go into the deepest ocean never to return. In Jesus' name. Amen.

Christians: Amen!

(Cockhiary lies still as if she is dead then she disappears).

ACT FOUR SCENE ONE

(Cockhiary goes back to her kingdom crying).

Cockhiary: Mama, mama, I was disobedient. Please forgive me I pray you.

Mallah: You are a disgrace to the spirit world. You have humiliated me. You have cancelled all your good works with this last deed. Consequences maintained!

(Exit).

ACT FOUR SCENE TWO

(Akele, Menke and Deaconess Fake meet the Pastor in his house).

Akele: Pastor, our God is faithful. All is now well at home. He came and searched for me and the children. He apologised and was so sorry. He now reads the Bible and prays regularly.

Menke: Same with me. He now loves me more than any woman; I believe.

Pastor: *(Laughs).* God is great. May His name be praised forever. He is omnipotent.

Fake: *(weeping)* I am very sorry pastor. It was in search of a child that I let my husband visit Ta Ngiri. After five months, I had that child, yet testified it was from God. I am very sorry, please forgive me.

Pastor: Don't be troubled, God listens to those who sincerely repent.

(Exeunt).

EPILOGUE

(The Narrator is relieved and speaks with much courage).

Narrator: Cockhiary has been overthrown. She is powerless. *(Pause).* What happened in her Kingdom? Demotion of course! She is stripped of her powers and position. Her shoulders have fallen in disgrace.

The Christians are stronger and more united than ever. There is no more immorality in the church. "Once beaten, twice shy".

Their God is omnipotent, omniscient, and omnipresent. He gives His children various gifts to help them in their warfare. He has fully equipped them.

THE END.